Code 7

Code 7

Cracking the Code
for an Epic Life

Bryan R. Johnson

CANDY WRAPPER INC.

CHICAGO

To my Jefferson, Talmage, and Genevieve,
I can't imagine a world without each of you.

TABLE OF CONTENTS

A World of Possibilities	1
Smash Mouth Taffy	15
Handle with Care	31
The Monster	45
Break a Leg	61
Oh Rats!	75
Code 7	87

Dear Reader,

You are invited to crack a code - one that will put you on the path to lead an epic life. Read this book closely. The Code is composed of seven important words, and if you learn to live by them, you will be prepared to become what you desire.

This book reveals the secrets of the Code. These are the stories of the first seven members who cracked it. They call themselves Code 7. More members have joined since then. I am one of them.

By the end, I hope you'll consider yourself to be a member too.

Now get cracking!

Bryan Johnson

1

A World of Possibilities

In the school auditorium, Jefferson sat with his fifth grade class as the students of Flint Hill Elementary filed in. It was near the end of the day, and he was ready to get out of school. He didn't think much of assemblies—lectures on bullying, school safety … boring. While he waited, he took a tiny notepad and pencil from his pocket and started to draw. Drawing was something Jefferson loved to do—second only to painting.

Jefferson's best friend, Darren, was sitting beside him. "What are you drawing this time?"

"The usual," Jefferson said. "What I see."

Jefferson sketched a picture of the scene before him. He drew in Principal Cooler, who was standing on stage with a large chalkboard behind her. He worked on her poofy hair and black-rimmed glasses.

Principal Cooler cleared her throat. "Students and staff," she began, "this year marks an important year for Flint Hill. Our school is celebrating its fiftieth anniversary!"

Principal Cooler politely clapped and the audience followed suit.

"But the school building is showing its age. It's time we address that."

A hundred whispers filled the room. Jefferson paused from his drawing, wondering what Principal Cooler had meant.

"They're going to tear this place down!" Darren smacked a fist into his palm. "Bam!"

"In your dreams." Jefferson knew that wouldn't happen. Flint Hill was proud, and the small town was even prouder. Some famous scientist who invented plastic—or something like that—went here. They'd never demolish the school.

Principal Cooler grabbed chalk from the tray. "Today I'd like to hear suggestions about how we can make our school look better than ever for our big anniversary celebration. Who has an idea?"

Dozens of hands shot into the air. Principal Cooler called on a second grade boy.

"Let's build a roller coaster that starts in the cafeteria and ends at the bus stop," he said.

"Roller coaster." Principal Cooler wrote the words on the chalkboard. "That might be a bit much, but thank you for your suggestion." She turned to face the audience. "Now what else would make the school a real standout?"

Jefferson thought about Flint Hill, sitting atop its grassy, manicured slope. The lawn always looked amazing because

Mr. Summers, the groundskeeper, had a knack for cutting perfect patterns with the riding mower in the grass. But the building itself was a miserable two-story rectangular shoebox in comparison. It had been painted in white over and over again to make it look new when it clearly wasn't. *Something that will stand out,* Jefferson thought.

Then it hit him. "A MURAL!" he blurted.

Everyone turned to look.

"We could paint something cool on the side of the building!"

"Like graffiti?" Darren said. "Sweet."

The audience buzzed with excitement.

"Isn't that illegal?" someone called out. "Awesome!"

Darren began to chant. "Mural, mural, mural!"

Jefferson elbowed Darren to stop him from causing a scene. But it seemed Jefferson's idea was taking over the room. "MURAL! MURAL!" everyone shouted.

As the teachers tried to quiet everyone, Principal Cooler thought it over. She waited until the room was calm and set down her chalk. "A mural is a brilliant idea! That would look great on the wall that overlooks the lawn and faces the town. It will transform the entire school. But who will paint it?"

"That's easy," Darren called out. "Jefferson can draw and paint anything."

Jefferson's ears burned. *Darren, quit it.* How could *he* do the mural? He wasn't an artist, like the real grown-up people who got paid to do that.

"It's true," said Katherine, a classmate sitting a row behind him. "Everyone knows Jefferson is a killer artist. Miss Baar is always using his work as an example in art class."

Jefferson swallowed. *She does?*

Miss Baar stood from the front row. "Principal Cooler, I have no doubt Jefferson can paint something perfect for the mural. He's a true artist. I'd say we put him in charge."

Jefferson gaped. *True artist? Put me in charge?* What had Miss Baar put in her coffee this morning?

But before Jefferson could refuse the job, Darren had started another round of chanting. "Jefferson! Jefferson! Jefferson!"

The decision was made.

After the assembly ended, the students were released for the day. Principal Cooler stopped Jefferson at his locker. "I can't wait to see your vision for the mural."

"My vision?" Jefferson mumbled as he tossed a few things into his backpack. "I mean, my vision will be great!"

Principal Cooler was all business. She opened the schedule book she was holding and ran her finger down the page. "Our anniversary celebration is in a month. I'm inviting the mayor, so you'll need to get started ASAP. Let's have an assembly next week to look at your plan." She slapped the book shut. "Sound good? Great!"

She spun on her heel and left Jefferson standing alone at his locker.

The mayor? A plan by next week? He slung his backpack over his shoulder and closed his locker. How was he going to do this?

He headed out the side entrance. Mr. Summers was riding the mower, doing his weekly cut of the lawn. Jefferson strode out onto the grass and turned to look at the largest canvas he had ever laid eyes on. The two-story white brick wall seemed to go on forever. What was he going to fill that with? How was he even going to get up there?

A few students spotted Jefferson before they got onto a school bus. "Do something cool," a boy said, "like snakes!"

"Paint a zoo," a girl said.

"No, superheroes!" suggested another boy.

As the kids boarded the bus, Jefferson thought about their ideas. Suddenly, he could picture something. A vision! He pulled out his notepad and jotted things down.

The following week, the school auditorium was noisy with excitement. Principal Cooler was already onstage. A screen had been set up, and Jefferson was standing behind a laptop. Once the students quieted, Principal Cooler said, "Jefferson will present his design idea for the mural. When he is finished, I will ask for your opinions."

Jefferson's hands started to sweat as he pulled up an image. "I hope you like it."

The auditorium got quiet as everyone took in Jefferson's design. There was a lot to look at—superheroes, a zoo, snakes, flowers, a roller coaster—practically everything that had been mentioned to Jefferson in the last week.

Finally, a kindergartener squealed, "The puppy I wanted is so cute!"

Jefferson sighed with relief. She liked it!

"But Sparkles really should be pink."

Jefferson's smile faded. He glanced at Principal Cooler, who was standing to the side. "Interesting," she said. Then she smoothed her skirt and faced the audience. "So? Raise your hand if you have feedback for Jefferson."

Dozens of hands shot up. One student suggested that Jefferson use different superheroes, another thought that he should add a motorcycle, and another wanted him to change all the colors to black and white. Jefferson bit his lip and scribbled down all their ideas.

"Not to worry," Principal Cooler said. "Jefferson has another week to come up with a revision. Assembly dismissed!"

After school, Jefferson went outside to look at the wall again, hoping to be inspired. He nodded a hello to Mr. Summers, who was mowing perfectly cut lines up and down the lawn. Jefferson turned to stare at his canvas. Only two stories of white wall. Yet he had enough ideas from everyone for a four-story wall! How was he going to design something that would work?

Ugh. He was just a kid. He wasn't a real artist!

Then it hit him. Of course!

He was just a kid, and all he'd been doing was listening to other kids. The teachers were the ones who made the rules at Flint Hill. He should find out what they would want, and then he couldn't go wrong.

The following week, everyone was gathered in the auditorium again. Jefferson knew this design would go off without a hitch. After Principal Cooler got everyone's attention, Jefferson brought up an image on the screen. There it was, Flint Hill—everything the teachers thought would represent the school best, suggested by the rule-makers themselves. Jefferson beamed.

Mr. Averett, the librarian, had asked for books. Ms. Mislavsky thought drama masks would be nice. Mrs. Mouritsen wanted a falcon, the school mascot. Jefferson even put in the cup of coffee Miss Baar said she really needed the other day.

"Oh my," Principal Cooler said, studying the screen. "I see you've also included an image of a bigger paycheck for Mr. Lu. Interesting. Um … anyone have feedback for Jefferson?"

Hundreds of hands shot up.

Principal Cooler picked a girl in the front row.

"Where's Sparkles?" she said.

"Yeah, what happened to everything *we* wanted?" said another student.

Many of the students were upset that everything they had asked for was gone. But the kicker was when Mr. Averett said he wanted the books on the mural to be arranged by the Dewey Decimal System, *not* alphabetically.

Jefferson's stomach sank. When he looked at his design again, he didn't see anything that had made him confident anymore. It was a disaster. The mural was not cool. How could he ever think a bunch of teachers' ideas could be great to begin with? What was he thinking?

But Principal Cooler remained as calm as ever. "Everyone, we put Jefferson on the job because he is a true artist, right? And Flint Hill is not just any school. We are a proud school.

We see the possibilities in everyone, and we see it with Jefferson, just like we did with the plastics inventor who went here fifty years ago. Let's give Jefferson the boost he needs." Principal Cooler did more polite clapping.

"I'm a believer!" Darren called from the audience. "Jefferson! Jefferson! Jefferson!"

Before long, the whole school was chanting. But this time, Jefferson wondered if they meant it, or if they just loved being able to shout in school without getting into trouble.

After the assembly was over, Jefferson strode out to the lawn again.

There was Mr. Summers, like an old friend, mowing that lawn and making the school look terrible in comparison. Jefferson groaned. Maybe it was Mr. Summers's fault that Jefferson was stuck in this mess!

Jefferson looked at the wall, lay down in the grass, and closed his eyes. His head was swimming with the ideas everyone had given him. From superheroes to poodles to library books, he'd drawn it all. There was nothing left to draw anymore. He closed his eyes, his thoughts spinning.

"Hey, boy," someone said.

Jefferson opened his eyes. He had no idea how long he'd been lying there.

Mr. Summers was standing over him. "I haven't mowed this spot yet."

Jefferson got to his feet. "Sorry about that."

Mr. Summers took off his cap and wiped the sweat from his brow. "You're the kid who's going to paint that wall, aren't you?"

"Supposed to."

"Good. It's making my lawn look bad. Make it perfect."

"If I only knew how. No one likes my ideas for it."

Mr. Summers scratched his head. "I'm confused." He pointed at the wall with his cap. "That wall is blank. Don't you have to paint something first? Where's *your* idea?"

Jefferson started to explain, but as he stared at the blank wall, something occurred to him. He hadn't painted anything. He'd been so busy listening to everyone else's ideas. Where was *his*?

Mr. Summers marched back to his mower. "Paint the wall, boy," he called back. "Then ask what everyone thinks. Now I've got a lawn to cut."

As Mr. Summers started the mower, Jefferson glanced at the endless slope of perfectly cut grass that the groundskeeper had already finished.

Paint the wall.

Mr. Summers was right.

Jefferson smiled and pulled out his notepad.

The next day, Jefferson told Principal Cooler what he wanted to do. She got him everything he needed: the paint, brushes, and a helper—Mr. Summers. To paint the wall, Jefferson wore a harness and worked on a platform supported by four large ropes hanging from the roof.

Mr. Summers would move Jefferson around the wall by using the ropes. Every day after school until the anniversary neared, Jefferson worked on his painting.

For the next two weeks, the only thing anyone talked about was Jefferson's mural. Everyone had guesses, but no one knew what it was because Jefferson had been carefully covering each completed section to protect it from the elements while it dried.

When the big day finally arrived, Flint Hill's fiftieth anniversary celebration was huge. Practically everyone from the town was there for the grand unveiling of the mural, including the mayor. They *had* to know what was on that wall!

Principal Cooler made a speech about fifty years of pride ... accomplishment ... achievement. Jefferson stood between the principal and the mayor. But being right next to the mayor didn't even faze Jefferson. All his thoughts were centered on the grand unveiling.

Finally, Principal Cooler said, "And now, Mr. Mayor, Flint Hill presents a mural that represents who we are as a school and the community we live in, designed and executed by one of our very own students. Jefferson Johnson, will you do us the honor?"

Jefferson walked to the side of the wall. He took in a deep breath and tugged on a rope that Mr. Summers had rigged for him. The cloth dropped.

One by one, everyone's eyes got big; jaws dropped.

The mural was beautiful. Awesome. *Cool.* Boys and girls alike started yelling and clapping. Principal Cooler beamed like Jefferson was actually *her* son, and not the son of Jefferson's real parents, who were standing in the front row, cheering their heads off.

Jefferson couldn't have felt more proud. He was an artist—a real artist with *vision.*

After the ceremony ended, Darren slapped Jefferson on the back. "So how did you know what to do, man?"

Jefferson shrugged. "The usual. I paint what I see."

Jefferson and Darren stared at the mural together.

Jefferson had painted a continuation of a perfectly cut, expansive green lawn that met a gorgeous horizon in the distance. The sky in the mural matched the real one behind it. At the top, Jefferson had written, "Flint Hill: See Your Possibilities."

Flint Hill looked like it just might be brand new and, like Mr. Summers's lawn, it was absolutely perfect too.

2

Smash Mouth Taffy

"But I really need the G-Force 5000," Sebastian said to his family over dinner. Practically every boy in school got the latest gaming system over the holidays, except him.

"I don't think that's a good idea, Sebastian." His mother scooped a helping of rice onto her plate. "We'd like to see you doing something more worthwhile with your time."

"Maybe you could take up something like soccer," his father said. "Like Jason."

Jason's freckled face lit up. "You can be on my team. Yay!"

Sebastian looked across the table at his Great-Aunt Martha, who always came for dinner on Wednesdays. "What do *you* think, Aunt Martha?" He made a pleading face at her, hoping she could help solve his problem.

Aunt Martha set down her fork. "I think Sebastian should earn the money to buy this system. Perhaps if he put his efforts toward doing useful things to earn it, he would deserve the benefits of having this G-Force Fifty thing."

Sebastian's parents glanced at each other. "Earn the money …" his mother said. "Sebastian could wash dishes, babysit—I love this idea."

"The lawn does need weeding," his father added. "The garage could use a cleanout. By the time Sebastian makes enough to buy the G-Force, our boy will be a changed man. He should be able to have what he wants if he shows us that he can be helpful too."

Smiling, Aunt Martha began to butter a roll. "I'm glad we could think of something."

Sebastian frowned. Babysitting, cleaning out garages? *Thanks a lot, Aunt Martha.* He'd rather eat pickles dipped in bug guts before he'd do all that. He pushed back from the table. "I'd like to be excused."

He went to his bedroom to sulk about how unreasonable the idea was. He tossed himself onto his bed. All he wanted was a simple gaming system—something everybody else's parents had no trouble getting. But no, he had to be stuck with a family who wanted him to be "helpful."

Someone knocked.

"Come in," Sebastian muttered.

Sebastian's door opened and Aunt Martha stepped in. Her old-lady handbag hung off her arm. "Did I say something wrong at the table, Sebastian?"

Sebastian sighed. "No, I'll be fine."

Aunt Martha sat on the edge of his bed. "I was only trying to be helpful."

"I know."

She opened her purse, reached inside, and pulled out a piece of taffy.

Aunt Martha always had a load of taffy in her purse. Ever since Sebastian was little, she'd been doling them out.

"This might not solve your problems," Aunt Martha said, "but my taffy will do you—"

"A world of good," Sebastian finished.

That's what she called the candies. The paper around the candy said as much, lettered in Aunt Martha's shaky handwriting. Sebastian undid the wrapper and popped the candy into his mouth. It melted easily with sweet yumminess. Instantly, he felt better.

"What's in these things?" Sebastian said.

"You know I can't tell you that, Sebastian. Your Great-Grandpa Nelson said the family recipe stays with me." She patted her purse. "This candy has been doing good for us for more than one hundred years."

"That long?"

"Indeed." Aunt Martha stood up. "Take a few for the road; it seems like you're going to need them." She handed Sebastian a plastic bag full of candy and left the room.

Sebastian stared at the bag. Then he closed his eyes and wished it were a G-Force 5000 instead.

The next day, all Sebastian's buddies at school could talk about were the cool games they'd been playing on the

G-Force. They talked about them on the bus, during lunch, at recess, and on the ride home. If Sebastian didn't get one soon, he'd be friendless by semester's end when his pals had figured out he was still stuck with his old system, playing a decade-old version of ping-pong. How was he going to get a G-Force and get it *fast?*

When Sebastian got home, he plunked down on his bed and grabbed a piece of taffy off his nightstand. He contemplated washing dishes for his mother. *Ugh! No way.*

"Sebastian?" Jason was standing in his doorway, dressed in his full soccer get-up. He was holding a box of chocolate bars. "Mom's taking me to the grocery store so I can sell these to passing customers. Wanna help?"

Sebastian unwrapped the piece of taffy. "Are you going to pay me?" He popped it in his mouth. *Man, these are good.*

"No, Sebastian. I'm supposed to take money, not give it away. Coach Newbury says if I sell this whole box, I'll have enough for my next tournament."

Sebastian grumbled. *I bet Dad and Mom love that Jason is earning his way toward soccer success by selling candy. How helpful.*

Wait a second.

Sebastian stared at the candy wrapper in his hand. "Jason, you're awesome."

Jason brightened. "You're going to help?"

"Nope." Sebastian got up and nudged his brother out of his room. "Good luck with that."

The very next day, Sebastian thought he'd try out his new idea on the school bus. As his friends went on about the hottest G-Force game they were playing, Sebastian slowly pulled out a piece of taffy. He unwrapped it and waved a hand over the candy so the scent of taffy goodness filled the air.

"What's that?" his friend Lincoln asked.

"Oh, nothing." Sebastian put the candy in his mouth. Then he closed his eyes and sighed with satisfaction as he chewed.

"Hey, man," Maddox said. "Share."

"Yeah," added Neal.

Sebastian held up a finger as he chewed some more and swallowed. "Can't." He pulled the bag of taffy out of his backpack. "I've only got this many. Spent my whole allowance on them. But if you've got a quarter, I'll give you one."

Within seconds, Sebastian had three quarters in his hand. That's when Sebastian knew: he was onto something.

The following Wednesday, Sebastian executed the next step in his plan. Over dinner, when Aunt Martha was busy talking to his mother about the latest in hairpin technology, he snuck a hand in Aunt Martha's purse and rummaged through it. His fingers closed around a tiny notebook. *Bingo.*

Sebastian set up shop in his tree house the next afternoon. He went over Grandpa Nelson's secret recipe, which was actually quite simple.

Butter, sugar, cornstarch, and vanilla.

By his rough calculations, he could make at least one batch per night, and he could unload them all on the school bus within a couple of days. He'd have a G-Force in just a few weeks, if things went well. He got out the Bunsen burner that he had swiped from the science lab, his mother's giant lobster pot, the necessary ingredients, and waxed paper from the kitchen. He went to work.

On the bus the next day, Sebastian's candy sold out before he made it to school. Even the bus driver, Mr. Steve, bought a piece. As Sebastian was about to get off, Mr. Steve stopped him. "What do you call this wonderful candy, son?"

"Aunt Martha's—I mean, er … uh … Smash Mouth Taffy!" *Sebastian, you're brilliant.* He smiled.

"Great name. Tomorrow, I'll take a whole bag."

A whole bag?

That's when Sebastian knew he could not do this alone.

At first, Jason was not the most enthusiastic assistant when Sebastian dragged him to the tree house and asked for his help. "Why should I help?" he said. "You wouldn't even sell my chocolate bars with me the other day."

But after Sebastian told Jason he could keep a dime for every dollar Sebastian made, Jason became the leanest, meanest taffy-wrapping machine anyone could find this side of the northern hemisphere. All weekend long,

Sebastian and Jason made hundreds of pieces of taffy and stuffed them into baggies that they had nabbed from the kitchen. Now Sebastian could sell the candy in bulk.

No one was the wiser. Sure, Sebastian's parents noticed that Sebastian had been spending an awful lot of time with Jason in the tree house, but they didn't bother to see what was going on. "Honey," Sebastian's dad said to his mother, "for once, our boy is playing outside with his brother and not obsessing about video games. I'd call that good."

When Monday came, Sebastian crammed his backpack full of candy. When he came down to breakfast, his mother handed him some money. "Buy your lunch today, sweetie. We're out of sandwich bags."

Jason was sitting at the kitchen table. Sebastian and Jason exchanged looks.

"I'll pick some up after I get Jason from soccer practice," his mother continued.

Sebastian let out a breath. Mom didn't have a clue.

That morning, Sebastian sold out of Smash Mouth Taffy before the bus made it to school again, and this time he took in a couple of bucks for every bag. When Sebastian and Jason counted up the money in the tree house that afternoon, they realized Sebastian was already a quarter of the way to getting a G-Force, and it wouldn't be long before Jason owned a new pair of soccer cleats.

For fun, they lay in the pile of spare change and dirty dollar bills.

"Boss," Jason said, "we need to make more money." He grabbed a bunch of quarters and let them trickle to the floor. "Lots of it."

Sebastian was thinking the same thing. Smash Mouth Taffy wasn't just a world of good anymore. It was a world of cold, hard cash. He knew that the only way to make more money was to get more hands on deck; he needed a full-blown operation. "I know exactly how we'll do it."

The following day, Sebastian called a meeting after school at the tree house with Jason and his three closest buds. He paced the floor as he filled everyone in on his plan. "Men, Smash Mouth Taffy isn't just a piece of candy; it's a way of life."

Maddox, Neal, Lincoln, and Jason all nodded.

"Forget Bus #54—we're going after the entire school," Sebastian ordered. "We're going to need more waxed paper. More Bunsen burners. More bags. More butter. More everything! We have to be careful; we don't want our parents to notice that things are missing. But … do what you got to do. Swipe whatever you can get away with. I want everyone here at 4 p.m. sharp tomorrow."

That very evening, extra baggies, sugar, and sticks of butter disappeared from kitchens. The boys toiled away in the afternoons, making candy.

Smash Mouth Taffy soon caught on like wildfire in the halls at school. Hardly a single kid could resist all that sugary goodness. By the end of the week, Sebastian had earned more than enough to get the G-Force, but he couldn't stop now.

Not when the world needed Smash Mouth Taffy.

It wasn't long before Sebastian's team had to take more extreme measures when supplies ran out. "Men, we need more capital," Sebastian said. "Get it!"

Soon, sibling piggy banks were raided to buy supplies. Then twenty-dollar bills disappeared from parents' wallets and purses. By the third week, it seemed to Sebastian that he wouldn't even need to stay in school if they kept making money at this rate. He was rich. Filthy stinking rich!

That is, until … a scream broke out in the school cafeteria. "Justin Tenuta has cooties!"

Not far away, Sebastian looked up from the candy deal he was making with a second grader.

"Cooties?" a girl said from another table. "That is so third grade. That's not cooties. That's *hives*."

"Hives?" Justin said. "I'm so itchy."

"Ohmigoodness." The girl began to scratch at her arm. "I've got them too. Did you give me cooties, Justin?"

"I thought you said I had hives."

"You can't have hives if you gave them to me just by sitting near you." The girl started turning pink. "Holy cow! You DO have cooties."

"Cooties!" someone else said dramatically. "Agh!"

Pandemonium broke out in the cafeteria. "It's a cooties outbreak!"

Everyone jumped up from the tables to get away.

"Don't touch me!"

"I think I've got them too!"

"Stop breathing on me!"

That day, approximately twenty-seven afflicted students were sent to the nurse's office, but it only took one Nurse Cratchet to identify the source of the epidemic.

She found a Smash Mouth wrapper in the pockets of nearly every single hive-infested student. "Where did you get this candy from?" she asked.

Everyone said, "Sebastian!"

In the principal's office, Sebastian had a lot of explaining to do, but he didn't even know where to begin.

No, he had no idea why the candy had given some of his customers hives.

Yes, he knew that stealing money was a bad idea.

No, he didn't know that his crew had swiped every Bunsen burner in the science lab and that the school had thought they had a real, bona fide break-in.

And no, he did not realize that more than a hundred people were upset with him, including his parents, everyone who broke out in hives, their parents, his friends' parents who had been stolen from, the siblings whose piggy banks were emptied, and even his three buddies who blamed

Sebastian for the whole thing because they were in trouble too.

To make matters worse, when Sebastian got home, Aunt Martha nearly fainted at the dinner table when she realized that the recipe had been stolen. "Oh, Sebastian, how could you?"

As they ate, Sebastian's parents lectured him about integrity, honesty, and every other moral value they could think of.

Sebastian could hardly listen. He only stared at Jason, who sat there innocently across from him as though nothing bad had taken place.

Then Sebastian realized that the only person who wasn't mad at him was his little brother.

Wait a second.

"It's Jason's fault!" Sebastian blurted, interrupting his parents.

Jason's face reddened. Suddenly, he burst into tears. "I didn't mean to, Boss. We ran out of vanilla, so I used Mom's almond extract instead."

"Goodness." Aunt Martha shuddered. "Grandpa Nelson's taffy is supposed to be nut-free."

"You enlisted your brother in this?" his mother said, horrified.

Sebastian's father was livid. "The school is a nut-free zone. You could have killed someone. You are grounded, mister, and you will not be getting any G-Force thingy EVER."

When Sebastian went to his room, he felt like he'd just eaten sweaty tube socks for dinner—awful.

A few moments later, someone knocked.

Sebastian sighed from his bed, hoping it wasn't his dad, ready to tear into him again. "Come in," Sebastian mumbled.

Aunt Martha stepped in, purse on her arm. "Sebastian, I just wanted to say good-bye for the night."

Sebastian sighed. He felt super guilty for stealing Aunt Martha's recipe. He opened the drawer to his nightstand, pulled out her notebook, and handed it back to her. "I'm sorry."

Aunt Martha patted Sebastian's hand as she took the notebook from him. "I know you are." She put the notebook in her purse. "I'm sure you didn't mean for this to happen."

Sebastian frowned. "Definitely not."

"You'll make this right, Sebastian."

"How?"

Aunt Martha reached into her purse and pulled out a handful of taffy.

"Take it." She placed the taffy in his palm. "This is all Grandpa Nelson ever wanted. Maybe it's something you will want too."

With that, Aunt Martha left.

Sebastian stared at the candy. While the taffy would taste great at the moment, he had a feeling Aunt Martha hadn't given it to him to make him feel better. This time was different. He read the shaky handwriting on the wrapper, and his hand felt heavy from the weight of the taffy.

A World of Good.

Sebastian swallowed.

He knew what he had to do.

The next day, Sebastian returned all the Bunsen burners and gave all the money they had made from the taffy to the people who had been stolen from, and then some. Smash Mouth operations officially closed, and Sebastian recorded zero profits.

Things slowly returned to normal, more or less. Sebastian's friends eventually got over the fact that they had gotten into trouble too, and they began to credit Sebastian for helping them rise to elementary school infamy for being a part of the scandal. Talk about Smash Mouth and the big cooties outbreak began to fade, and his friends started discussing the latest video games to hit the market.

Sebastian saw the world differently, though. After Smash Mouth, the talk about video games suddenly didn't have the same kind of appeal anymore.

Maybe he was ready to make things right—not just for other people, but also for himself.

When Sebastian got home, he went to the kitchen.

A bunch of dirty dishes were stacked in the sink.

He pushed up his sleeves and got to work.

And just like Aunt Martha's taffy, washing dishes felt good—a world of good, now that he was a part of it.

3

Handle with Care

Monday, Genevieve's homeroom teacher Miss Skeen held up an egg at the front of the classroom. "Class, this is our project for the week."

Genevieve's eyes widened. She smiled. She knew what this project was about. "I can't wait!" she chimed in. She dreamed of becoming a veterinarian, and now she was going to hatch a real chick.

"Let's fry it up," Josh said from across the aisle.

Genevieve frowned. Josh always made a joke of everything. This was an innocent life in the teacher's hands—not breakfast.

"Not today," Miss Skeen said. "You will each take care of an egg for seven days."

Juliet, Genevieve's best friend, groaned from the next row. "A whole week. That's, like, forever." But to Genevieve, it wasn't long enough. Surely it would take more than that to incubate an egg.

Miss Skeen held up a large carton. "I got these at the grocery store, and I've carefully inspected each egg—"

"The grocery store?" said Theo from the back. He always questioned everything and knew practically everything. "Miss Skeen, store-bought eggs are sterile. A live chicken is not coming out of that."

"You're right, Theo." Miss Skeen returned the egg to the carton. "The point of this project is to learn a few things about life, not the life cycle."

"The eggs won't hatch?" Genevieve said, disappointed.

"No hatching," Miss Skeen confirmed. "Instead, I want you to learn what it's like to care for something—or 'someone' in this case—and what better way is there than using an egg that is fragile and helpless? Treat your eggs as if they are your children. Give them names, take them wherever you go, and record your experiences. If, for any reason, you can't take care of the egg, you may have someone else egg-sit, like parents do when they can't be with their kids."

She began to hand out the eggs. "No matter what, you are responsible for the egg. Your eggs are specially marked with my stamp and will be inspected in class every day. If the eggs are scratched, nicked, or punctured in any way, I will deduct points from your final score. If the egg is broken or mysteriously replaced, you will receive no credit."

Genevieve jotted down everything Miss Skeen said. Though she was bummed that she wouldn't be hatching a live chick, she still liked the project. If she was going to be a vet, she would take good care of her egg in need. This would be a test—one she was determined to pass. When

Miss Skeen gave Genevieve her egg, she held it gently in her hands and named it Chloe.

Everyone made baskets for their eggs out of cardstock, pipe cleaners, and cotton balls. Genevieve built her carrier extra strong, reinforcing the sides and sticking in twice the amount of cotton balls for padding. She labeled the carrier *Chloe* and colored the cotton balls pink.

Josh pretended to gag at Genevieve's basket. "You are taking this way too seriously."

Genevieve rolled her eyes just as homeroom was dismissed. She proudly carried Chloe everywhere—to her classes, the water fountain, and the cafeteria. As she sat next to Juliet at lunch, an egg went flying past her head.

Josh and his buddy Calvin were playing a game of toss over Genevieve's table.

Genevieve and Juliet looked on in horror.

"Are they crazy?" Juliet said.

Calvin missed Josh's egg, and "Hulk" dropped to the floor. Splat! "Oops!"

But instead of getting mad at Calvin, Josh only shrugged. "Guess that's a zero for me." Calvin and Josh laughed.

"Boys," Juliet said. "I'd never let them babysit my egg." She patted her egg. "You'll be safe, Leona," she cooed.

Genevieve agreed with Juliet as she scooted Chloe closer to herself. "Yeah, one of those boys egg-sitting would be a disaster."

As the week wore on, more eggs succumbed to care-lessness and mishandling. Dan's egg fell out of his bike basket when he went over a bump. Aaron's egg was eaten by his dog, Shark. Even Claire's egg got cracked when she took it to the mall.

By Friday, only half the eggs were still okay, including Genevieve's egg, Chloe. "Last night," Juliet said at lunch, "my brother tried to play tennis with Leona. This project is driving me nuts. Leona will never survive my horseback riding lessons this weekend!"

Genevieve felt bad for Juliet. Taking care of her own egg hadn't been all that hard for her. "Maybe … I could take care of Leona for you," Genevieve offered.

Juliet brightened. "Really? You're the only one I can trust. You're so good with Chloe!" She gave Genevieve a hug. "I'll pay you with chocolate, I promise."

"No need. Just drop her off at my house tonight."

Suddenly, Genevieve's whole table was swarming with classmates. "Did I hear that you're going to babysit Juliet's egg for free?" Ethan said. "Take Tiger for me." He thrust the egg in her face. "I'm going to ride a roller coaster tomorrow, and there's no way he'll survive that. I couldn't trust him with anyone but you."

Genevieve looked at poor, innocent Tiger with a bandage on his head. She couldn't say no. "Okay, bring him to my house tonight by seven."

"Deal!"

By the end of lunch, Genevieve became the official egg-sitter for almost everyone in the class who still had an intact egg. Genevieve didn't mind. She cared about those eggs; they would be her little patients. She knew she could do it, and it would be a win-win for everyone.

When Genevieve went to science class, Theo stopped by her lab table.

"Drop off your egg by 7 p.m.," Genevieve whispered as she studied an amoeba through a microscope.

"Actually," Theo said, resting his egg carrier beside Chloe's, "don't you think you're making a mistake egg-sitting for everyone?"

Genevieve looked up. "What do you mean?"

"You're going to take care of all of those eggs, including your own, for three days? Shouldn't you focus on Chloe? You're getting taken advantage of."

Genevieve went back to her microscope. "Technically, Theo, it's only two and a half days. Monday morning, everyone will get the eggs back. And I'm perfectly capable of taking care of more than one egg." Then she eyed Theo suspiciously. "And why do you care anyway?"

"Just thought I'd point out the obvious," Theo replied. "Well, if you're going to keep the eggs, maybe I can help."

"You? Help?" Genevieve said. Why would Theo want to do that? Then something occurred to her. "How come you aren't giving your egg to me?"

"Why should I?" Theo said. "I've been spending the whole week trying to figure out how to hatch my egg into a chick."

Genevieve was confused. "But you said the eggs were sterile. Why would you try to do that?"

"Because … " Theo glanced away, his face turning red. "… because I want to be a scientist," he blurted.

"Scientist?" *Theo doesn't need to be embarrassed about something like that,* Genevieve thought. "I see."

"Never mind then." Theo picked up his egg. "Clearly, you have this covered. Forget I asked." He walked back to his table.

Genevieve peeked over at Chloe. "We don't need Theo's help, do we?"

That evening, fourteen eggs arrived at her doorstep to receive proper care from Dr. Genevieve. She built a special carrier for them out of a milk crate and egg cartons, careful to label and note the condition of each egg upon arrival. All weekend long, she got the eggs plenty of exercise and fresh air by taking them to the park in a stroller. She talked to them for company and sang them songs to keep them entertained. She even read them bedtime stories before lights out.

When Genevieve walked into homeroom on Monday, she felt like a hero. She carefully placed the crate of eggs on her desk and set Chloe down beside it. Her classmates gathered around and tried to retrieve their eggs, but Genevieve waved their hands away. "It's the last inspection! Don't touch them. You don't want something to happen now, do you?"

Juliet withdrew her hand like she'd touched a hot stove. "Good point."

"Genevieve," Miss Skeen said from the front of the room, "why don't you walk everyone's eggs up so I can check them?"

"No problem," Genevieve said proudly. She firmly gripped the handles of the crate and headed toward her teacher, knowing that because of her excellent care, these eggs would make it to the end of the project. As Genevieve walked up the aisle, she was wondering if she would get extra credit for doing such a great job when, suddenly, she tripped on something and the crate went flying.

Oh no!

The eggs flew through the air.

Genevieve caught herself on Theo's desk. The eggs!

Crack! Crack! Splat! Splat! Splat!

Everyone gasped.

Miss Skeen was a goopy, eggy mess! "Goodness gracious!"

Genevieve could hardly look.

Miss Skeen was covered in egg yolk and runny whites. Genevieve turned to see what had tripped her. There was nothing in the aisle, but Josh was at his desk with his hands folded in front of him. He looked like a cat that had just swallowed a mouse.

He had tripped her. She just knew it! "JOSH!"

Josh's face looked surprised. "What?"

Apparently no one had seen Josh trip her.

"Genevieve, you tripped on purpose, didn't you?" Ethan said. "I knew I shouldn't have trusted Tiger to a girl!"

Juliet came to Genevieve's defense. "That's crazy. She'd never do that on purpose."

"Yes, she would," Calvin joined in. "Why do you think she took care of our eggs for free? She had this planned all along."

"Class!" Miss Skeen tried to get everyone's attention, but no one listened.

"I didn't plan this!" Genevieve retorted.

But everyone ignored her. "You're right, Calvin." Josh got up and pointed at Chloe. "Look whose egg is still perfect. Genevieve's egg!"

"Class!" Miss Skeen called again, but everyone ignored her. They were all too busy watching five boys rush Chloe.

No! Genevieve couldn't stop them. In seconds, Chloe was in midair, dangling from Ethan's fingertips. "Now *you* can see what it feels like."

"Ethan, don't you dare!" Miss Skeen warned.

But he did. *"Sayonara!"* Chloe dropped from his fingers.

Genevieve squeezed her eyes shut.

Ping!

Ping? She opened her eyes. Chloe was bouncing off the floor, like a plastic ping-pong ball would.

Ping! The egg bounced again before coming to rest in front of Calvin's feet.

The whole class gasped again.

"That's not an egg!" Josh said.

Calvin grabbed it from the floor. "It's plastic! You're a CHEATER!"

Genevieve was stunned.

Theo shook his head. "I told you not to trust them."

"CLASS, THAT'S ENOUGH!" Miss Skeen was shouting now. She shook a runny finger at them. "No one say a word!"

Everyone got quiet.

Miss Skeen straightened and attempted to smooth her goopy hair. "Genevieve, Josh, Ethan, Theo " She then rattled off the names of the other boys who had all tried to get Genevieve's egg. "Everyone, to the principal's office!"

When they arrived, Principal Cooler whirled around in her chair to stare at everyone. "What's this I hear about an egg fight breaking out in the classroom?"

Immediately, Josh explained his conspiracy theory about Genevieve, blaming her for the entire egg disaster and calling her a cheater. As Josh talked, Genevieve sat quietly, afraid to speak. She'd never been in trouble like this before; she could hardly think! What had happened to Chloe? Why did Josh have to trip her? How could people be so mean, despite everything she had done to help them?

"Is that so, Josh?" the principal finally said after listening to the boy's tale. "Seems to me that I've seen you and some of you other boys about a dozen times, but Genevieve has never gotten into trouble. Am I right?"

Genevieve nodded.

The principal turned her attention to Theo. "And what is your part in this, Theo? You're usually on my honor roll, not in my office."

"I swapped Genevieve's egg for a plastic one."

Genevieve's jaw dropped. Theo took Chloe?

"And where is her egg?"

"It's safe in my backpack in homeroom. I was going to return it to her before inspection, but I never got the chance."

The principal scratched something down on a notepad. "Now why would you do such a thing, Theo?"

Genevieve turned to glare at Theo. *Yeah, why?*

Theo shrugged, looking just as awkward as he had in science lab. "No reason, really."

Genevieve sighed. Maybe Theo had gone off the deep end.

The principal set down her pen, frowning. "Theo, seeing that this is your first offense, and that there is no rule against the swapping of dairy products, you will return the egg to Genevieve immediately, and you'll receive a written warning. And Josh, it appears you are wrong about Genevieve. I suspect she also didn't fall on purpose, either."

Josh swallowed. After the principal gave the other boys detention, they were dismissed. Theo tried to follow Genevieve down the hall. "Let me explain." But Genevieve didn't want explanations. She sped up. She wanted to get away from everyone, especially Theo. The egg project was supposed to be fun and meaningful. But at that moment, she couldn't care less!

That evening, Genevieve sat in her room, trying to do homework, but she kept staring at Chloe's empty basket. She missed having an egg with her, even though no one else seemed to care. It was all a joke to them. Genevieve then wondered if something was wrong with her. Why did she have to care so much? Maybe it shouldn't matter to her either.

The doorbell rang. Genevieve pushed back from her desk. "I'll get it!" When she opened the front door, Theo was standing there. His bike was resting against her front porch.

He held up an egg in a new box filled with straw. "Please, will you just take Chloe?"

Genevieve crossed her arms. "Why should I? The project is over."

He held the box up to her face.

"Chloe needs you."

Genevieve stared at her egg, and she felt something twinge in her heart. It was good to see Chloe again. But she still couldn't ignore the fact that the whole egg ordeal bothered her. "Cut it out, Theo. It's just an egg, like everyone says."

"It's not just an egg," Theo said.

"Oh, yeah? Then tell me why you took it."

Theo looked away. His voice was barely audible. "Because I care."

"What?" Genevieve said.

"Because I care, all right?" he said more firmly. "Just take it, will you? You'll understand." He shoved the box into her hands. "Keep her warm. If you've got a desk lamp with a high wattage bulb, that'll work."

Genevieve was confused. "Okay," she mumbled. Maybe Theo really had gone off the deep end.

Theo grabbed the handlebars of his bike and turned to leave. "Bye."

"Bye."

Genevieve took the egg inside and carried Chloe to her room. She turned on her desk lamp. Under the glow of the light, Genevieve noticed that her egg had a hairline crack running along its side. Was the egg moving?

A note was resting in the straw. She unfolded it.

I'm the scientist. You're the vet. Now see what you can do with this.

Genevieve peered at the egg again. "Chloe?"

The egg moved.

That night, Genevieve watched baby Chloe break her way out of her shell. As she looked at something so tiny and innocent emerge from its protective home, what the other kids thought didn't seem to matter anymore.

She looked at the baby chick, peeping with new life.

Maybe she and Theo weren't that different after all.

She cared.

That's all that mattered.

4

The Monster

"Time to wake up!" Talmage's father called from the hall. "We have an appointment with the Monster."

Talmage stretched in his bedroom and squinted at the clock. It was six in the morning and the first Saturday of the summer. It was time to go fishing for the Monster, something he'd been doing with his dad every summer for as long as he could remember.

His door opened. Dad tossed a snack bar onto his bed. "Breakfast. Let's go."

After Talmage got dressed, he headed out back, where Wallamaloo Lake awaited them.

Dad was on the dock, loading the old motorboat. "Conditions are perfect. Today is the day—"

"I can just feel it," Talmage finished. He smiled. His dad always said that.

Suddenly, Dad's face turned serious. "Today is the day, Talmage." He brought his special fishing rod onboard; it was the deep-sea fishing kind, especially meant for the

45

Monster. "Twenty years ago, I swore I'd get him, and I will." He gave the barrel of the rod a pat.

Talmage took his place on the rear bench. "You think we're finally going to catch him?" He surveyed the dark, murky water around him.

"I have to." Dad pushed the boat away from the dock.

Talmage had never seen his father look more determined to catch the mysterious fish. Legend had it that the Monster was big enough to eat a dog. It could jump fifty feet out of the water and overturn a boat. The stories were so embedded in everyone's mind that no kid dared to swim in the lake without saying a prayer before jumping in.

None of the stories bothered Talmage or his father. "He's a beast, all right," Talmage's dad had once said. "But he's no killer. When I had him on the line, I stared him right in the eye, and all I saw was fear."

According to his father, that fish had bent his pole like a paper clip and nearly yanked him out of the boat before the line broke. All around town, people knew of the story. To believers, his father was sorta famous for being the only person to see and hook the Monster.

"We'll get him, Dad," Talmage said with equal determination. But deep inside, catching the Monster didn't matter much to Talmage; he just loved their fishing trips. There was something special about being on the lake with his father before most of the town woke up.

Talmage could eat all the junk food he wanted, listen to good music on their old radio, and just sit without a care in the world. Dad did most of the real work when it came to the fishing part.

Dad started the motor and switched on the radio. The oldies station was playing the Beatles. "Perfect." Dad grinned. "Talmage, the weather is hot. The Monster loves his water warm. We couldn't have asked for better conditions."

They motored out to the spot where the Wallamaloo River dumped into the lake. "He likes the action of the water," Dad explained. "Keeps the food marching right into his big mouth."

Once Dad cut off the motor, he got his line ready. Already there were a few boats out, trolling for their own catch of the day. Talmage recognized Leonard and his son Paolo's fancy motorboat several hundred yards away. Dad tipped his fishing hat in Leonard's direction. Leonard tipped his hat in return.

"That Leonard is going to eat my bait," Dad said under his breath, "when the Monster is on my dinner plate tonight."

Talmage held back a laugh. Dad always called his old high school classmate "that Leonard," even though everyone else called him Leo. Leonard was known for being the best sportfisherman around. Last year he and his son caught the biggest muskie that the state had ever seen. But to Talmage's father, the fifty-eight-pound fish they hooked still wasn't the Monster.

All day, Dad cast and recast his line, but as the hours went by, the fun day Talmage had hoped they would have wasn't so fun after all. Dad had hardly said a word. It was like he had pinned all his hopes on catching the fish that very morning. To make matters worse, they didn't get a nibble from anything at all, which was unusual. Talmage wiped the sweat from his brow. Maybe it was too warm to fish. He glanced at his watch. It was past noon; usually they quit for lunch and waited until dusk to head out again. Some of the other boats were already heading back, including Leonard's.

"Bryan!" Leonard called to Talmage's father as they coasted by with the engine rumbling. "Just a tip—it's the radio. You're chasing away the Monster with that music."

"You fish your way," Dad called, "and I'll fish mine."

Just then, something tugged on Dad's line, *hard.* Dad held it fast and started reeling. "See?" he said to Leonard. His pole jerked again. "I've got a big one! Help me, Talmage."

Talmage stood up. "What should I do?"

The pole jerked forward once more.

Leonard stopped his boat. "You need me, Bryan?"

"We've got this." Dad reeled the line as quickly as he could. "Just hold onto my waist, Talmage." He bent the pole back to get some power over the fish. "He feels huge, bigger than I remember."

Talmage grabbed onto his father and planted his feet in the decking.

"He's putting up a good fight!" Dad bent the pole back again.

Sure enough, whatever Dad had was rising to the surface. It was big—a dark gray mass about three feet wide coming toward the boat. Talmage's eyes widened. What was that?

Dad tugged and reeled, tugged and reeled.

Talmage dug in with his heels.

"On one, two, three—PULL!"

Talmage pulled on his dad as hard as he could.

He lost his footing and his father landed on him. Something big came out of the water. *The Monster,* Talmage thought.

Bang! A giant tire hit the side of the boat before sinking under with a splash.

Talmage heard peals of laughter from Leonard's boat. His face flushed red.

His father scrambled to his feet and cut the line with his pocketknife.

Talmage sat up, rubbing his back. That was no Monster.

"Stop laughing, Paolo," Leonard warned. "It's not funny."

But Talmage could tell that Leonard was holding back his own chuckle. The man revved the motor to a roar. "We'll see you later, Bryan." With that, they sped off.

Talmage's dad dropped his pole and took off his hat. He chucked the hat to the deck.

Talmage stared at the hat, and then he looked at his father. "You okay?"

Dad took a few seconds to compose himself. "Yeah." He looked at the horizon and finally picked up the hat. "We're heading home." He yanked on the motor pull.

That evening, Dad didn't say much. He sat in the living room in his tattered wingback chair, staring at the empty fireplace like it was a TV set.

Talmage tried to cheer him up. "Come on, Dad. It was Leonard's loud and obnoxious boat that ran the Monster off. We'll get him tonight. I just know it."

His father didn't say anything.

Talmage began to worry; he'd never seen him this down over fishing. "Dad?"

"Talmage," his father began, "you know my story about the Monster, right?"

"You said it was the best day of your life," Talmage recalled. "No one had ever done what you had—hook the Monster."

"Right," Dad said. "It was the best day of my life. I had the right weather. The right tackle. The right fishing spot. I had taken Grandpa's boat out all by myself."

Talmage nodded, remembering the details of the story.

"But I never told you that day was also my worst. Grandpa didn't believe me when I told him I had hooked the Monster."

Talmage frowned. His own dad hadn't believed him?

"And I saw the way Leonard and Paolo looked at us today. It wasn't just me they were laughing at. It was us."

"Who cares?" Talmage said. "We're catching the Monster, Dad. You had him, and I believe you."

Dad's face grew stern. "Talmage, it's over. Trying to catch a fish I haven't seen in twenty years is impossible." He shook his head. "Impossible. Now I sound like Dad."

Talmage stared at his father. He didn't like to see him act this way.

"The funny thing is," Dad continued, "when I had the Monster on the line, the radio was playing Grandpa's favorite song. I remember wishing so badly that he could have been there with me. What a moment we would have had!" He began to sing.

"You put the hours in and the day is done; it's quittin' time. But when it comes to getting what you want, from the moon to the sun, you never give up. You never give in.

"Grandpa wasn't a believer in the Monster, like some of the townsfolk here. But to his credit, he was a big believer in me. He taught me to never give up in life—to go after what I wanted."

Dad got up from the chair. "And I wanted that fish. But it's time to stop. I'm not going to let you follow in my footsteps. Not this way." He sighed. "I give up." He ruffled Talmage's hair and headed to his bedroom. "Night, son."

That evening as Talmage lay in bed, he thought about what his father had said and how sad his father had looked.

Talmage made a silent vow to the Monster and to his father. His dad had given up, but he hadn't. He was going to catch that fish, once and for all, and he spent the entire night thinking about how he was going to do it.

On Monday, Talmage pretended to sleep while he waited for his dad to go to work. As soon as Talmage heard the front door shut, he jumped out of bed with a notebook in his hand. He got dressed and grabbed everything he needed from the shed where they kept the fishing supplies. He loaded the motorboat and headed out.

When he arrived at the mouth of the river, he opened his notebook and looked over a matrix he had drawn. Three columns were labeled *Bait, Location,* and *Weather.* Each row represented a time of day. He knew Dad had always tried to fish for the Monster by looking for conditions that were similar to the day his father had hooked the fish. But after twenty years, Talmage figured it was time to try something new. What if the fish didn't like Dad's lure anymore or preferred a different spot? Talmage figured if he noted the weather and methodically changed the variables that he could control, like the bait and the location, he would eventually discover the right combo and nab that fish. Talmage filled in the first row in the matrix: *Chartreuse Crankbait, Mouth of River, Warm and Sunny.*

For company, Talmage switched on the radio. He adjusted his baseball cap and cast his line. If anyone was going to catch the Monster, it would be him now that he had "the system." Talmage smiled.

That month of June, Talmage tried different lures at all times of day at the mouth of Wallamaloo River. He grabbed every chance he could to fish, usually when his father was at work, fast asleep, or out for a ride on his motorcycle (something his dad did a lot since he gave up on the Monster). By the end of the month, Talmage's notebook was one-third full of entries, but still no Monster.

Nevertheless, Talmage's determination didn't flag. He still had dozens of locations to try. Talmage began fishing at Quarry's Cove, Gillman's Point, and Wheaton's Dock. He swapped out the lures and fished in all sorts of weather: rain, wind, and scorching heat.

Still no Monster.

By the end of summer, the notebook looked beat up; it was full, and Talmage was beginning to wonder if he was meant to catch the fish after all. On the last weekend before school began, Talmage sat on his bed and mulled over the entries in his notebook. Was there any combination he hadn't tried?

His father knocked, and then the door opened. "Talmage, have you seen my fishing pole?"

Talmage quickly closed his notebook. *Dad's pole.* He had been so eager to get to bed last night, he hadn't put it away. It was in the boat. "Um … no."

His father scratched his head. "I know I stored it in the shed ages ago. But it's not there. I wanted to sell it."

"Sell it?"

"Yeah." A flicker of sadness crossed his father's face. "No sense in keeping it. Someone must have taken it." He sighed. "It's just as well."

After Dad left, Talmage stared at his notebook. He didn't know how much longer he could stand seeing his father miserable over the Monster. He opened the notebook and studied the last few pages again. He had to find a way. As he scanned the entries, a new possibility came to him. Talmage's heart sped up a little as he thought it over.

There was one more combination he hadn't tried.

That evening, when his father was asleep, Talmage went out on the boat, more determined than ever. He motored out to the mouth of the river and threw on Dad's old lure. He never thought to use Dad's lure and go to the same old spot. What if it wasn't the bait or the location, but the fisherman? Dad had said the fish had looked scared of him. But the Monster didn't know Talmage. It was worth a try.

Talmage flipped on the radio and cast his line. He waited patiently, knowing that this was his last hope. Over and over again, he cast his line and reeled it in. Hours went by with the stars twinkling above and eventually Talmage couldn't ignore the sinking feeling growing in his stomach. He began to hate fishing, the Monster, and his vow to catch the fish. A Beatles song came on the radio, and it instantly brought Talmage back to the day that he and his dad had caught a monster all right—a monster of a tire! *Funny how a song can bring you right back to the moment,* Talmage thought. Paolo's laughter. Dad chucking the hat. He'd never forget that day. It had started out great, and then it quickly became one of the worst days of his life. Just like the day his father had hooked the Monster. What a curse!

Talmage straightened. *Wait a second.*

Just like the day his father had hooked the Monster.

He reeled in the line and turned on the motor. He had to get back to the house. Quick.

He burst through the door of his father's bedroom. "Wake up, Dad! We have an appointment with the Monster!"

His dad sat up in bed and squinted at Talmage. "What are you talking about?"

Talmage tugged at his father. "We have to try one more thing."

"Talmage, what on earth?"

But Talmage wouldn't let his father stay in bed. He wouldn't let him give up. He made him get dressed and dragged him outside. "Today is the day," Talmage said. "I just know it!"

The sky was still dark, but soon it would welcome dawn. "Hurry, Dad! It's almost six."

As Talmage started the boat, he made his father look at the notebook. Talmage filled him in on the way to the mouth of the Wallamaloo River. "See, Dad? All summer, I've been trying every possible thing to catch the Monster. But we know the Monster isn't some ordinary fish, yet we've been acting as though he thinks and behaves like one. That doesn't make any sense!"

His father listened as they went to the spot where they usually fished.

"He's not any old fish attracted by regular old lures." Talmage cut off the motor and pointed at the radio. "What was that song, Dad? What was Grandpa's favorite song? Sing it!"

Talmage's dad stared at Talmage in disbelief. "What?"

"Sing the song." Talmage tried to remember the words. "Something about the moon and the sun."

Talmage's father stared at his son. "Oh, what do we have to lose?" He looked at the deep, murky water. The moonlight shone over its surface.

He began to sing.

"When the hours are in, and the day is done; it's quittin' time. But when it comes to getting what you want, from the moon to the sun ... "

Talmage joined in. "... you never give up. You never give in."

The lake grew eerily quiet. For a moment, it seemed like the lake was listening.

"Again," Talmage whispered.

"When the hours are in … " they sang.

The boat suddenly began to shift. Small waves formed in the water.

"Talmage?" his father said.

Talmage kept singing. "Get the pole, Dad."

"We don't need the pole," his dad said. "I think he's coming right to us."

Talmage stared at the growing ripples in the water. His father was right. "Keep singing," Talmage whispered. Neither of them dared to move.

" … From the moon to the sun … "

The ripples grew even larger. The Monster was coming.

"You never give up … "

Something began to rise from the surface, just as rays of sunlight hit the water.

Talmage could feel the boat rise from the force of the waves, and what emerged was bigger than anything Talmage could have imagined. He swallowed. " … you never give in."

And then he saw it. The Monster's brilliant emerald green head. The dark orb of his eye.

The eye was so big Talmage could see himself and his dad in its glassy reflection. Talmage could hardly breathe, but he wasn't scared.

Neither was the Monster.

"There you are," Talmage's father whispered.

Then as quickly as the fish had come, it slipped into the water with a splash that echoed across the lake. The boat rocked from its wake.

Talmage and his father stood in silence as the lake grew still again.

Then Talmage realized something dreadful. "Dad, we didn't catch him."

His father put his arm around Talmage's shoulder. "It's okay."

Talmage stared at the spot where the Monster had been. "Who's going to believe us?"

"It doesn't matter," Dad said. "I got what I wanted."

Talmage wrinkled his face. "No, you didn't."

His father looked at him. "Talmage, all I wanted to show you was that if you don't give up, anything is possible. But you know what?"

"What?"

"You just did that for me instead." He gave Talmage's shoulder a squeeze.

With those words, Talmage gazed at the lake again. His father was right. It was one of the best days of his life, and the deep, murky water of Wallamaloo Lake was as clear as it could ever be.

5

Break a Leg

rs. Huff tacked up a poster in the hall outside the school auditorium. Eager students in the drama club gathered around. "It's official," Mrs. Huff said, facing everyone. "Our musical has been chosen. Tomorrow, I'll hand out scripts so you can practice for auditions next week. Good luck!"

Samantha stood on her tippy-toes to look at the poster, but Trista, one of the tallest girls in the club, was blocking her view. "We're going to do *Little Shop of Horrors!*" Trista exclaimed to her friends.

Yes! Samantha loved that story. It was so full of hope, so full of dreams.

Samantha's best friend, Reina, seemed just as excited. "Wardrobe for that will be fun." Reina always did wardrobe; she wanted to be a fashion designer one day. "What about you, Samantha? Tell me you're trying out for a part."

Samantha's enthusiasm quickly faded. She bit her lip. *Should I try out this time?*

Trista spun around. "Why would Sam try out for anything?" She put an arm around Samantha. "We need her to be a stagehand like last year. Right, girls?"

One of Trista's friends nodded. "Who's going to move the set around and fetch us water?"

"Yeah," another friend added. "Plus, we'd like to keep the show accident-free, if you know what I mean," she smirked.

Samantha's cheeks burned. No one would ever forget about what had happened the last time she starred in a musical. *Ugh.*

"Besides," Trista added, "my dad says if I get the lead, he's going to fly in Mr. Mason, a big talent scout from New York, to see me perform. You wouldn't ruin that opportunity for me, would you, Sam?"

Samantha swallowed. Trista's father was the mayor, and Trista could really make Samantha's life miserable if she didn't cooperate. The last student who dared to ruffle Trista's feathers had to move out of town; the pet dog was suddenly declared a noise disturbance, and the family wouldn't give him up. At least, that was the rumor.

Samantha sighed. "Of course, I won't ruin it for you."

Trista smiled with satisfaction. "I thought you'd agree, and my girls will take the chorus parts, right?" Her voice got louder so everyone standing nearby could hear. "Right?"

Everyone nodded.

"Then it's settled," Trista said. "You and the others will be supporting staff. We'll handle the rest." Trista sauntered off with her friends.

"The nerve," Reina said. "Playing 'politics' to get her way. It's disgusting."

"It doesn't matter," Samantha said. "I wouldn't have tried out anyway."

"Why not?"

Samantha stared at Reina. "Hellooo, who can forget that I, Samantha Shannin, cancelled the entire school's performance of *Annie* because Annie—me—fell off the stage and screamed bloody murder over a fractured tibia? I singlehandedly gave the phrase 'break a leg' a whole new meaning."

Reina frowned. "That was two years ago."

"I know," Samantha said. "But I also like doing the stagehand stuff too, so it's fine. Really." Sort of.

Reina raised an eyebrow. "Is that so? Being a stagehand is not why you're in the drama club, and you know it." She turned to leave. "I'll see you tomorrow."

After Reina left, Samantha walked home, thinking about what Reina had said. Her friend was right. The whole reason she was in the drama club was because she loved theater and everything about it, but what she wanted most of all was to sing in a musical. She had dreamed of Broadway since she was big enough to hold a hairbrush for a microphone and throw a feather boa over her shoulder.

Samantha stopped in the middle of the sidewalk and imagined herself as Audrey, the lead, singing "Suddenly Seymour." The crowd would be dazzled. But the next image she saw was herself falling into the orchestra pit. *Crash!*

As she shrieked in agony, trying to extract herself from the timpani drum, Trista would be looking down at her, hands on hips. "Audrey should have been *mine*." Then hundreds of kids would flock to the scene and whip out their cell phones, snapping pics of Samantha's little mishap.

Samantha's vision faded, and the neighborhood came into view again. Try out for Audrey? *Forget it.*

The next week at auditions, only Reina dared to challenge Trista for the lead, but she didn't get the part. Reina couldn't sing a note if her Christian Lecroix vintage purse depended on it. Later that day, Reina and Samantha hung out on Samantha's bed in her room. "At least I tried," Reina said. "Someone has to take the she-monster down. I think Mrs. Huff is dying for anyone besides Trista to play the lead. You should have auditioned—you would have beaten her."

Samantha shook her head. She wasn't ready to face Trista's wrath if she had gotten the part. "It's just not my time, but at least you get to be an understudy. That's a step."

Reina grinned. "I bet Trista can't stand that. Why don't we get sick and cough on her a few days before the show? Then when she comes down with a horrible case of strep, I can take the lead and put Trista in her place."

The idea was appealing. But … "It's just not worth it. She'll be a fine Audrey."

Reina tossed a pillow at Samantha. "You're driving me nuts! Don't let Trista take away your dreams. You're scared of her."

"No, I'm not."

"Yes, you are."

The truth was Reina was sorta right. Samantha was worried about Trista, but what Reina didn't know was that she was more worried about messing up the whole show. She just couldn't bring herself to do that again, dream or no dream.

Over the course of the next two months, the club focused on the production of their new musical. As the weeks went by, it irked Samantha more and more that Trista had the part. She was just so mediocre. She couldn't remember her lines. She would always get the blocking messed up, and she danced like a gangly giraffe. Samantha felt sorry for Mrs. Huff. Her teacher always looked like she would rather wallpaper her bathroom than coach Trista through her part.

To make matters worse, Reina was having a tough time being an understudy. Not only was Samantha working on the set design, but she was also helping Reina rehearse in the evenings.

"Why did I try out for Audrey?" Reina moaned. "Now I'm thinking Trista better not get sick or I'll make a fool out of myself."

"It'll be fine," Samantha said. "You've got the blocking down. Your lines are almost memorized. The only thing that's messed up is the singing."

Reina threw up her hands. "This is a nightmare. I'm going to get Trista back for being so mean."

"Is that so?"

"Yes, I am." She narrowed her eyes. "Wait until you see the outfit I've picked out for her. She'll totally love it."

Sure enough, just before dress rehearsals the following week, Reina presented Trista with her wardrobe selection. "I can't wear that outfit!" Trista complained. "It looks so used … and wide … and frumpy!"

"The show has practically no budget," Reina explained. "I had to make do with whatever we already had in the theater department. They're your size, and they'd be perfect for Audrey's part."

"My size?" Trista clutched the potato sack of a dress. "These stripes will make me look huge. I'll do my own wardrobe, thank you very much." She tossed the dress at Reina.

Mrs. Huff stopped her work with Eric, the boy who was playing Seymour. "Trista, wear what Reina chose.

I'll have no prima donnas on my set; you're not in Holly-wood yet."

"But Mrs. Huff," Trista protested, "I can't wear used clothing. I could have a severe allergic reaction."

Mrs. Huff let out a slow breath. "Get a doctor's note."

Trista smiled. "I will." And the next day, she did.

She also came back with a new outfit to wear. Samantha had to admit the leopard print dress and fur stole looked great for the part. "Mom had it custom-made." She held up a pair of insanely tall matching pumps. "They're designer. Made out of real leopard. Can you believe it?"

Everyone gawked. Reina stuck her finger down her throat.

By week's end, the club was ready for dress rehearsal. After listening to Trista warble the music for weeks, Samantha couldn't wait for the show to be done. The pressure of Mr. Mason coming to town was also making everyone nervous. Mrs. Huff didn't want anyone to mess up. Eric was nervous, the chorus was nervous, even the kids controlling the man-eating plant were making the plant shake too much.

As Samantha worked on the finishing touches for a set piece, Mrs. Huff stepped off the stage while Trista and Eric practiced a duet. She rubbed her temples like she was having a migraine. "Samantha," she said, lowering her voice, "why couldn't you have tried out?"

Had Mrs. Huff completely forgotten that Samantha had single-handedly destroyed an entire musical? "Um … Trista is much better than I would be," Samantha stammered.

Mrs. Huff glanced back at Trista, who was trying to dance and sha-la-la at the same time. "Are you sure about that?"

Samantha swallowed. "Uh-huh."

Just then Eric's voice cracked.

"Well," Mrs. Huff said, "there's nothing to fear but fear itself. All of my students need to learn that. Including those two."

Samantha nodded.

"Do it again, Trista!" Mrs. Huff called. "It's supposed to be a shuffle-step, not the polka."

Samantha watched Mrs. Huff return to the stage. She was so glad she wasn't up there.

The next evening, everyone geared up for the big performance. Reina was running around in the dressing room, helping Trista and her posse get ready. Samantha leaned against one of the lockers, wondering how long everyone was going to take. The show would be starting soon.

"I can't believe my zipper broke," one of Trista's friends whined. Even Trista was looking a bit off. Her eyes were tearing up and she was clutching a tissue. *"Aaaaachooo!"*

Reina's eyes bulged as she tried to fix the zipper. "Trista, you don't have a cold, do you?"

"Hardly," Trista said with a stuffy nose. "I'm allergic to my clothes."

Samantha and Reina stared at her. "What?"

Trista gestured to her dress and raised her leg, pointing her shoe in the air. "Allergic to leopard. Can you believe it? The doctor just figured it out yesterday. I told you I was allergic to stuff."

She rubbed her eyes and blinked a few times. "But the show must go on!" She stood up. "I'll be fine."

Reina looked frazzled. "Samantha, she better be fine. I'll die if I have to take her place."

Five minutes before showtime, Samantha and Reina peeked at the audience from the wings. The school musical was one of the town's biggest events. Every seat in the house was taken. With that many people there, Samantha wondered if she should have auditioned. She longed to sing to a packed house.

Her heart felt a tug of regret.

Reina seemed to know what Samantha was thinking. "One day, you'll sing."

The lights dimmed and the music started.

Eric moved onto the stage to act out his first scene as Seymour. Then Trista showed up next to Reina and Samantha. She wiped her nose. "How do I look?" she whispered.

Reina and Samantha stared at her. Trista looked awful. Her stage makeup was completely destroyed. Mascara ran down her cheeks, and her nose was as red as Rudolph's. *"Aachoooo!"*

"Shhh! You should probably change," Reina whispered. "I'll give you the clothes off my back so you can get out there."

"No need," Trista said, waving her hand as if to shoo Reina away. "Mr. Mason has to see a star on the stage, and I can't be seen wearing your rags. My outfit is what Audrey would wear, and that's who I am tonight. For Mr. Mason."

She waited for her cue, and then she tottered out to the stage in her heels.

"Could she be more obnoxious?" Reina said.

"Aachoo!"

Samantha shook her head. "I can't look." It made her sick to see Trista ruin a great show. She retreated backstage and waited for the first act to play out so she could help with the next scene change.

Everyone managed to make it to intermission without much incident. But when Samantha saw Trista in the wings, she doubted the girl was going to last through the whole play. Her eyes were bloodshot. She had gone through half a box of Kleenex. Everyone wondered if she needed a medic.

"I'm an actress," Trista said vehemently. *"Aachoo!* I won't give up over something like this. "

"Trista," Mrs. Huff said, "you clearly have a medical condition."

"Please, Mrs. Huff, I can do this," Trista insisted. "I'm totally fine. I won't let Mr. Mason down."

Reina stepped in. "Mrs. Huff, you gotta let her go on that stage." She crossed her fingers behind her back. "This is her dream."

"Oh, all right," Mrs. Huff relented, and Trista went out again.

"Just a few more numbers," Reina whispered to Samantha, "and I'm home free."

They watched as the duet for the song "Suddenly Seymour" began.

Trista's voice was growing hoarse, but she was still able to croak the lyrics. Samantha found herself admiring Trista for being so determined, even though she was making a hot mess of the show.

Suddenly, Trista stopped singing. She pursed her lips and squeezed her eyes shut as if trying to hold something back.

Uh-oh. What was she doing?

"Aaaaaaaachhooooooo!" Trista sneezed so hard she stumbled in her heels. She fell off the stage.

The crowd gasped. Samantha's heart skipped a beat as Trista crashed into the orchestra pit.

Was she hurt? Samantha and Reina rushed down the stage steps toward her.

"I'm fine!" Trista shouted immediately. She sprang up from the pit. Her dress was torn and her hair was sticking up everywhere. "I'm fine!" She plucked a violin bow out of her hair. "See?"

The crowd let out a collective sigh of relief as the lights came on. The audience showered Trista with applause, glad she was safe.

Mrs. Huff hurried to help Trista.

"I can still do it, Mrs. Huff," Trista pleaded. "Pleaasssse! I can finish the show. I haven't broken a leg or anything! DADDY! MR. MASON, ARE YOU SEEING THIS? I AM STILL GOING ON! I'M A TRUE STAR!"

But Mrs. Huff wasn't having it. She led Trista out of the pit as fast as she could. As she passed Reina and Samantha, she said, "Reina, it's showtime. Get up there."

The lights dimmed again, and the crowd settled down.

"No way!" Reina hissed. "I can't do this. You go."

Samantha looked up at the stage. "Seymour" was just standing there, alone, looking like he was desperate to get out of the musical himself. The crowd was silent. Samantha bit her lip. The open stage was beckoning to her, but her insides spun with nausea. She was scared. What had Mrs. Huff said? There was nothing to fear but fear itself.

Samantha swallowed. Then, suddenly, she was tired of being afraid. Her hands clenched into fists. She couldn't give it any more power. That stage was meant to be hers.

She moved toward the stage and climbed the steps.

Someone noticed who she was. A boy shouted, "We always loved you, Sam!"

"Yay, it's Samantha!" shouted a girl.

Samantha stood a little taller. Maybe the audience had forgotten what had happened two years ago. Or … maybe she was the only person who had not.

More people cheered for her. She noticed a man in a fancy suit, sitting front row center. *Mr. Mason.*

Samantha stood beside Eric and took in a breath.

Maybe this was her time now.

She waited for the music to begin, and she sang.

She belted out the tune like it was the first and last song she would ever sing.

As the crowd rose and cheered her on, Samantha was that little girl again, singing into a hairbrush with the feather boa over her shoulder.

She was finally at home.

At home on the stage. Full of hope. Full of dreams.

She would never be afraid to go after her dreams again.

6

Oh Rats!

When Alec came home from school, his father called to him from his study. "For the twentieth time, Alec, please clean your room! Your mom and I have other things to do, like taking care of the baby."

Alec groaned as he dumped his backpack in the foyer. "I'll get to it, Dad."

But Alec never got to it. Why should he? His mother always did it for him anyway. He had other things to do, like hanging out with his friends. Even plucking his eyelashes out, one by one, would be more enjoyable than cleaning.

"Son, you need to show some responsibility," his father warned. "Your mother won't keep cleaning up after you anymore."

Alec shrugged and went to the kitchen. He doubted Dad really meant it. He grabbed a banana from the counter and went to his room. To prove his point, he smiled at the respectable mess, ate the banana, and dropped the peel to the carpet. *Just wait and see.* Then he went outside to find his friends at the park.

What Alec didn't know was that his father really did mean it. That very evening while Alec slept, his parents quietly discussed their son's fate in their bedroom. "The boy has no respect for authority," his father said. "Not a modicum of responsibility."

"I agree," his mother said as she placed a sleeping Serena in her crib. "If not him, then who? If not now, then when?"

"Without a doubt."

"I know what we need to do … " His mother let the words hang in the air and smiled.

"What?" Alec's father leaned in as she laid out her plan.

They were going to do something unthinkable, unimaginable—unspeakable!

They would do … absolutely nothing.

When Alec awoke, the scent of banana drifted to his nose, and he wondered if his father was making banana pancakes. He grinned, stretched, and plucked a dirty sock off his T-shirt. Blurry eyed, he got out of bed to get ready for the day. As he crossed the room, he slipped and fell to the floor. *Ugh!*

To Alec's surprise, yesterday's banana peel was still lying out. Hmmm. Perhaps Mom hadn't gotten to her regular room inspection yet. He peeled the banana from his foot, got up, and laid the peel nicely on the floor again.

When Alec returned home from school that day, the house was eerily silent. Alec peeked down the hall. "Dad?"

"Yes, Alec?" his father called from his study.

"Just checking." Usually someone would ask him to get to something right when he came in. He went to his bedroom and opened the door.

That was odd. The banana peel was still on the floor. "Mom?" Alec called.

"What is it?" his mother suddenly replied from the neighboring room. Alec flinched from surprise. His mother stepped into the hallway with baby Serena, who was sucking a pacifier, on her hip.

"Why does my room still look the same?" Alec asked.

His mother's face drew a blank. "Were you expecting something different?"

"Um … " He couldn't very well say that he was hoping his mother had picked up his room. "No. Everything's fine. See you later, Mom." Confused, he stepped inside and shut the door.

As he surveyed the mess, he crossed his arms and tried to figure out the perplexing situation. Then it came to him. He knew exactly what his parents were up to. *This meant war.*

For the next week, Alec not only let his mess grow, he went out of his way to make it worse. He knew that there would be no way his neat-freak mother and watchful father could stand to see Alec's room turn into a disaster. Naturally, they would have to give in first.

But what Alec didn't know was that his parents had already seen worse from their children—vomit in cars, urine on the walls, and blowout diapers. Piles of dirty clothes, food crumbs, and rotten banana peels didn't faze them.

Alec still refused to pick up his room. If he did, he would upset the balance of the universe. In Alec's mind, things like the cleanup of bedrooms were better left to the people who did them best. His mother was great at it; he was not. If he picked up after himself, he would be sending the wrong message; his parents might actually believe he was capable of such a task, and then things would really change.

So Alec continued to sully his living quarters to a reprehensible state. It got so bad that Alec had to hurdle piles of clothes and junk just to make it to his bed. The stench of rotting bananas began to mix in with the odor of moldy cheese. Even Alec could hardly stand the smell, so he opened the windows for some fresh air. He stuck his head out the window and smiled. Problem solved.

Another week went by. Since his parents still hadn't lifted a finger, Alec dirtied his room with a vengeance, thinking his parents would surely cave when trash began to flow out of his window and into the yard.

Word spread among his friends who had caught a glimpse of Alec's mess from the bus stop.

"Dude, your room is an epic disaster!" one commented.

"I can't believe your parents don't make you clean that," said another. "*Lucky.*"

"You should post a video of it to the Internet," said a third. "It's inspiring."

His friends wholeheartedly supported his cause. If Alec won the battle against his parents, they vowed they would do the same thing themselves and end all room-cleaning for good. Hearing this, Alec felt a surge of pride.

But the next week came and went. Instead of being magically clean, Alec's room looked like it needed to be quarantined in a self-contained bubble to prevent the spread of communicable diseases. On top of that, Alec had run out of clean clothes. Before he resorted to re-wearing his dirty stuff, he rescued really old clothes from the depths of his closet. Problem solved again, even though his Batman pajama bottoms were cutting off his circulation.

A week later, Alec began to hear scritching sounds coming from under his bed at night. *Scritch, scritch, scritch!*

Alec tried to ignore it and closed his eyes to sleep. But the sounds persisted. *Scritch! Scritch!*

He snapped on a pair of headphones and smiled. Once more, he'd found the perfect solution to the problem. Now he only had to endure the feeling of tiny rodent feet skittering across his chest while he slept.

Not long after, things changed at last. The phone began to ring off the hook. Neighbors complained to Alec's parents. Rats had been seen streaming in and out of Alec's bedroom window.

Alec quietly picked up the phone and eavesdropped.

"My wife is thinking about serving ratloaf for dinner," a neighbor said. "You must stop this at once."

Alec grinned. His parents would have to fix this at last. If not them, then whom? If not now, then when?

To Alec's complete astonishment, his mother and father did ... absolutely nothing.

What Alec didn't know was that his parents had been through much worse—his father's family had escaped from a war-torn country. His mother filed their taxes every year, without an accountant. A bunch of rats scurrying in and out of their house didn't faze them.

Soon enough, the neighbors grew angrier. Alec's family was reported for city violations. When large birds and stray cats began to circle Alec's home to hunt the rats, a concerned citizen appealed to Animal Control. But nothing could be done to make Alec clean his room. While Alec's parents could be held responsible for damage to other people's property, the city could do nothing if the rats and other animals were only interested in Alec's room. Also, according to the current municipal code, even flocks of birds and droves of cats could not be removed from private

property if the animals were indigenous to the town. The city certainly couldn't arrest stray felines for mewling on fences or flying fowl for pooping on the neighbors' heads. The city's hands were tied.

So Alec's parent's continued to do absolutely nothing!

Alec's friends cheered him on. Classmates wore T-shirts that read, "Get your mess on!" Others wrote a song called "Dirty is Purdy!" to show their solidarity. Still others carried rubbery gray rats with them to demonstrate that they, too, could live in peace with these adorable creatures.

"Dude, I wrote about you as 'My Hero' in English class," said a classmate as they passed in the hall.

But despite the support, Alec wondered exactly how long he could wake up in the morning to several large hawks staring at him from his bedpost.

Outraged by the city's inability to stop a growing catastrophe, the neighborhood began to picket. By the fifth week, Alec's messy room made the five o'clock news and the front page of *The Bugle:* "City Hall Needs a Cleanup to Clean Up Boy's Room." Embarrassed by the publicity, City Council called an emergency meeting; new laws would have to be passed to persuade Alec to clean up his room and prevent another situation like this from happening again.

The next day, a letter was tacked to Alec's front door.

PUBLIC HEALTH NOTICE

Due to recent events, City Council has begun a new government initiative aimed to protect the health and safety of our citizens—C.L.E.A.N. (Children Living, Eating, and Acting Neatly).

C.L.E.A.N. inspectors will be conducting random inspections of children's rooms. If a room is declared messy, C.L.E.A.N. inspectors will issue a verbal warning and demand the room be cleaned within twenty-four hours. A second violation will result in the forfeiture of one month's allowance to C.L.E.A.N. Upon receiving a third violation, the child will be grounded in his or her home and issued a standard orange jumpsuit. Activities will be limited to completing extra homework and potty breaks chaperoned by C.L.E.A.N. personnel.

Any child who is cited for a violation will be required to perform forty hours of cleaning training, which will include, but is not limited to, vacuuming, home organizing, and toilet bowl scrubbing.

This Order is hereby in effect as of TODAY.

Yours in Cleanliness,

City Council

Alec gulped. Things were really about to change, but not for the better.

His phone rang off the hook again. This time, every kid in town was calling to yell at him.

"Way to go, Alec!" one complained. "Why couldn't you pick up after yourself like you're supposed to?"

"Someone in a gas mask is bluelighting my underwear drawer right now," said another. "How could you do this to us?"

"Alec, I'll never forgive you!" said a third. "Orange is soooo not my color!"

As Alec listened to every angry call, he stood in his bedroom and watched baby Serena play in a pile of his litter. It was only a matter of time before C.L.E.A.N. inspectors would arrive.

Just then, Baby Serena's paci popped out of her mouth and landed in the pile. She grinned.

A siren went off and six men in protective suits invaded the room.

Alec's pride over the state of his room quickly faded.

Was this what he wanted?

For other people to take care of it?

He looked at the sea of trash, a wallaby-sized rat gnawing his way through the pillows, and the men who were sweeping Serena for parasites.

Was this what he wanted for his baby sister's future?

He had his answer.

That day, Alec began to clean up his room, but unfortunately he couldn't finish within the allotted time—his room was too far gone. Alec had plenty of time to think about what he had done during cleaning training, while he fluffed pillows and polished a toilet bowl under close supervision. Still, Alec marched onward and never failed another inspection.

But what Alec didn't know was, to his parents, a clean room was only the first of many things that were about to change in his life.

"Honey," Alec's mother said to her husband, "I think it's time that Alec understand that we are not going to finish his homework for him anymore."

Alec's father smiled. "Without a doubt."

7

Code 7

During homeroom, Kaitlyn listened from her desk as Principal Cooler made an announcement over the loudspeaker.

"I look forward to this week every year," the principal said. "Imagination Week is about imagining the world as a better place and then making it happen. I love team projects–this year is no exception!"

Kaitlyn sighed. The thought of a team project made her uncomfortable. She placed a hand on the messenger bag resting in her lap. Since moving to Flint Hill from New York City a year ago, she hadn't tried to get to know anyone. She preferred to keep to herself.

" … Teams will be assigned today; you will need to come up with a team name and get started on your plans. The winning group will get a pizza party for their class."

A collective cheer rang throughout the room. No one could resist a pizza party.

Katilyn's teacher, Mr. Loh, called out names, dividing the class into three groups of seven. Kaitlyn slung her bag over her shoulder and moved to the rear of the room to join her team. She didn't know any of them well, but she thought the Sebastian guy had caused a scandal at the school by selling bad candy. *Great.*

"Let's get started," Sebastian said. "We need to delegate tasks to the right people if we wanna go big. Trust me. I know from experience."

"What's the rush?" Alec interrupted. "We haven't even decided what we're doing yet." He looked at Jefferson. "Jefferson, come up with an idea everyone likes."

Jefferson swallowed. "Me?"

"You've done it before. Everyone went gaga over your mural."

"No, no," Talmage said. "Let's start with our own ideas first. I'm sure we can come up with something if we think about it long enough."

"I've got it," Samantha said. "We could put on a talent show to raise money. I could sing for a cause."

"I like it!" Genevieve said. "Maybe our cause could be about animals. What do you think, Kaitlyn?"

Kaitlyn bit her lip. "A talent show sounds okay." *So long as I'm not in it.* She wasn't sure she even possessed a true talent.

"Hold on a sec," Sebastian said. "Who wants to prance around on stage for a cause?"

"Even *I* wouldn't do that for a pizza party," Alec added.

"Me either," Talmage said.

"How are we going to make the world a better place?" Jefferson asked. "We need a cause. That's the point of Imagination Week. We could do something to support artists. Practically all of them are starving, you know."

"Agreed," Samantha said. "Singers are artists too. A lot of them resort to singing on the streets."

"What about the cats and dogs?" Genevieve asked. "So many are starving and living on the streets. They're helpless."

"Genevieve has a point," Alec said. "There are a lot of hungry, homeless animals out there. I know from experience."

"No, no … " Sebastian said, lost in thought. "We have to give small businesses a leg up. Now there's a cause."

Talmage piped in. "I know! We should do an obstacle course with all sorts of crazy challenges."

Everyone stared at Talmage.

"Why would we do that?" Alec asked.

Talmage lit up. "Because it's a cool idea?"

As the group debated ideas, Kaitlyn watched the conversation ping-pong back and forth. She wished she could point the video camera in her bag at all of them and capture the process. As the discussion went on, each teammate only became more convinced of his or her idea. "Without art," Jefferson said, "the world would be a very ugly place."

"But what about music?" Samantha said.

"Cats and dogs," Genevieve argued.

Sebastian paced the floor. "But businesses are the fabric of our community."

Talmage kept pushing the obstacle course idea.

Kaitlyn sighed again. There was no way this group could decide.

"What about you, Kaitlyn?" Genevieve said. "What do you think?"

"Um … " She had no idea what they could do. "Maybe we should spend the week working on something we each like." That would buy her more time. "Then on Friday, we can vote for the project we'll present on Monday."

Everyone looked at each other.

"That's genius," Alec said.

"Great idea," Samantha agreed.

"I don't see why not," Sebastian concluded. "One last order of business, we need a team name. Any thoughts?"

Decide something else? *Forget it.* "Why don't we wait on that name until we know what our project is?" Kaitlyn offered.

"Makes sense," Jefferson said.

"All in favor say aye," Sebastian said.

"Aye!" everyone chimed, just before the class bell rang.

Kaitlyn smiled. She had gotten what she wanted, a non-team project. But she still had a big problem. What was she going to do for her project? As she sat in her room that evening, she pulled the camera from her bag and rested it on her desk. She knew that it would involve her camera, but she didn't know what she would film. She didn't even have a cause, like "save the dolphins" or "find a cure." She filmed people because she loved the small stories that unfolded in front of her camera, like the time her old best friend told her on camera why she had the biggest crush on Chad Rice. Or when she filmed her cousin's high school graduation ceremony and caught the tear that slipped down her uncle's face. Or when Mom received an honor for documentary filmmaking. How powerful she had looked behind that podium, making a speech. Kaitlyn touched the camera.

What would Mom say? Mom always filmed important things. "Things that would change people's minds about the world," she would say.

Could Kaitlyn do that? What would she change people's minds about?

She didn't know, but she knew she had to start filming something. The next day, Kaitlyn met her group in homeroom. She had a proposal. "Does anyone mind if I video you doing your projects?"

"Video?" Alec said. "I don't think stealing our ideas is the way to go, Kaitlyn."

"That's not what I mean." She reached into her bag and pulled out her camera. "It's my project. I want to make a film. Maybe capturing you all working on your projects for a cause is my project?"

Genevieve's eyes lit up. "That's so cool, Kaitlyn. You know how to work that?"

"It looks fancy," Samantha added.

Kaitlyn blushed. "My mom gave it to me. She showed me how."

"I don't care if you film me," Talmage said.

"So long as you get my good side," Alec added.

Everyone agreed to allow Kaitlyn to film them. That day after school, Kaitlyn went with Jefferson to a local bus stop. She recorded with her camera as they walked.

"I want to transform how the town looks," Jefferson said, gesturing all around him. "All of our bus stands are neglected. We could decorate each stand with art, and hire local artists to complete them." Kaitlyn was impressed. It was a great idea.

Next, she met with Alec at the park. "My idea is to beautify the city by asking citizens to pick up after themselves and each other. We leave recyclable trash bags at various locations. So if you feel inclined, you can grab a bag, pick things up, and go. It'll teach everyone that the city's mess is everyone's responsibility."

When Kaitlyn met with Samantha at her house, she filmed Samantha working on a new song. "I want to sing something that will make people care about our world."

The following day, Kaitlyn captured Genevieve using a neighborhood map to establish a system of foster homes for pets. "If every kid at Flint Hill Elementary took an animal in, we could save hundreds of cats and dogs every year!"

Sebastian was drawing up business plans with his little brother, Jason. "I'd like to help small businesses attract more customers through low-cost advertising."

"We could have businesses sponsor my soccer team!" Jason added.

Talmage was building an obstacle course in his yard, complete with climbing walls, ropes, and a mud pool. "I'm going to stick random prizes in the mud that people will have to fish out. It'll be almost impossible to find the magic prize."

Everyone had such great ideas. Kaitlyn worried her project wouldn't seem nearly as good as everyone else's. All she had were random clips of her teammates. What kind of project was that?

Nevertheless, she kept filming because that was what she was drawn to, like some people draw or write. But as the week wore on, things started to fall apart for her teammates. Kaitlyn filmed Jefferson's disappointment as he realized he couldn't do the artist cooperative; starving artists had to be paid, and Jefferson didn't have the money. Samantha was having a severe case of writer's block when she discovered that Stevie Wonder and U2 had already done songs like hers. And Sebastian was pretty sure his business plan might be illegal if he was hoping to use the likenesses of famous athletes on company-sponsored soccer shirts.

When Kaitlyn went to film Genevieve, Genevieve had lost hope for her foster care system. About one-quarter of the student body had a household member who was allergic to dogs or cats. Another half had parents who already had enough to do with their own children's pets, and the other quarter would rather foster iguanas and tarantulas. The only teammate who seemed happy with his project was Talmage.

"We can't pitch an obstacle course because it's *cool* to Principal Cooler," Sebastian said in homeroom on Friday. "We've got to think of something important."

"What about you, Kaitlyn?" Alec said. "You've got something, right?"

Yeah, videos of disappointed teammates, Kaitlyn thought. "Not really."

"But this was your idea," Jefferson said. "To do our own thing separately."

"We let you film us," Samantha said.

"You can use that somehow, right?" Genevieve said, hopeful.

"I say we vote to submit Kaitlyn's project," Sebastian said. "Everyone in favor say aye."

"Aye!"

It was unanimous.

"We know you will think of something brilliant," Jefferson said. "Just see the possibilities."

"Meeting adjourned," Sebastian said.

Kaitlyn left homeroom with the team project resting heavily on her shoulders. Her plan to buy more time had completely backfired. What was she going to do now?

"Wait up!"

Kaitlyn turned in the hall.

Genevieve caught up to her. "You'll need my help."

"No," Kaitlyn said. "I've got it."

"You sure?" Genevieve looked uncertain. "I know we voted for your project, but you don't have to do it alone."

"Thanks," Kaitlyn said. "But I'm okay." She didn't want to involve anyone even more. She'd done enough already.

"All right," Genevieve said. "Call me if you need me."

Kaitlyn nodded. Genevieve was so nice. It was like she was built that way. So caring. If only Kaitlyn had cared as much, maybe she wouldn't be stuck in this mess.

When she got home from school, she loaded everything from her camera onto her computer. What could she change people's minds about? She played through every clip, but it was Genevieve's clips that she watched and rewatched.

Kaitlyn paused the playback on an image of Genevieve's disappointed face when she had learned her project wouldn't work. It was almost as though Genevieve believed every homeless dog and cat depended on her, and she'd let them all down. That was Genevieve's story, so easily captured in thirty seconds of film. Genevieve was always trying to help someone or something.

But what was Kaitlyn's story? Kaitlyn glanced at her reflection in her full-length mirror. She didn't like what she saw—the sadness from her mom's passing and then having to move away. For a year, Kaitlyn had kept her distance from other people because she didn't want them to see that too. She was sure everyone thought she was just a loner. But Kaitlyn wasn't a loner. She was just ... lonely.

Kaitlyn stared again at Genevieve on her computer screen. Genevieve cared enough that she offered to help Kaitlyn. Genevieve made her feel not so lonely anymore.

She thought about Imagination Week. Building a better world. She wanted to help Genevieve help those dogs and cats. She reviewed the clips of the others again and tried to focus. She filmed people because she was drawn to their stories. Jefferson's was about artistic vision. Samantha's was about her desire to sing. Talmage loved a good challenge. Alec wanted people to take responsibility for themselves and each other, and Sebastian embodied entrepreneurial spirit. Slowly, a larger story came to her mind—one that was much bigger than all of them combined. *What if ...*

That was it!

Kaitlyn immediately contacted her teammates and laid out a plan. Then all weekend she filmed her teammates working on her idea for their new project and edited the film.

Come Monday, Principal Cooler called an assembly for Imagination Week. Presentations went by grade level, and Kaitlyn's team was scheduled to go last. Kaitlyn could hardly sit still. First, the kindergartners came up and acted out a play where they reimagined a world where circle time was required for everyone to promote peace. The crowd went wild with applause. There were projects about poverty, education, and curing diseases. By the time a fourth grade team presented a thoughtful project about staying green, Kaitlyn's stomach was full of butterflies. Finally, it was time.

"And for our last presentation," Principal Cooler announced, "Kaitlyn Williams will be presenting for her team."

Kaitlyn went to the podium and held a notecard on which she had written a brief speech. She took in a breath and remembered how powerful her mother had looked when she had made her own speech.

"Imagination Week is about betterment of the world," Kaitlyn said. "I've learned that one person alone can only do so much. But when we share our stories and work together, we can do so much more." She cued up the film.

A sweet song sung by Samantha played over the loudspeakers. Images of puppies and kittens found on the streets of Flint Hill played on the screen. The audience aww-ed. Then Jefferson came on the screen. He was standing on an ordinary street. "Art has the power to beautify our community." Alec was next, talking about plastic bags and cleaning up the city. The next shot was Sebastian standing beside the owner of a pet supply shop. "People like Nate Romano keep our citizens employed and our animals fed." The screen went black; words flashed across the screen.

Ideas.

Become.

Reality.

The audience saw footage of Nate and his employees in the parking lot of Nate's Pet Supply. Large murals of cats and dogs, created by local artists, captured the attention of passersby. The lot was filled with an obstacle course for dogs and cats and handy poop-pickup stations for cleanup. Flint Hill citizens were checking out animals brought by Animal Control for adoption.

Genevieve held a Chihuahua in front of the camera. "Animal Control needs our help. Adoption events at Nate's Pet Supply save homeless cats and dogs. Your adoption fees and donations give our furry citizens the homes they deserve. Adopt a pet at Nate's next Adopt-a-Pet Event!"

More words and images flashed across the screen as Samantha's song played its final verse.

Individuals.

Work.

Together.

Next was an image of Jefferson helping artists with their murals as the word "Authenticity" appeared on the screen.

Another image came up: a picture of Sebastian shaking hands with Nate and the business council of Flint Hill. The word that appeared was "Character."

A snapshot appeared of Genevieve talking with an Animal Control official as shelter animals looked on. "Care."

Alec setting up pick-up stations with Nate's staff. "Responsibility."

Talmage training a retriever to jump over a hurdle. "Perseverance."

Samantha performing her song for attendees of the event. "Courage."

Then there was an image of Kaitlyn with her camera pointed at the adoption event.

Her word was "Become."

Kaitlyn spoke again as more images of homeless dogs and cats appeared on the screen. "These words tell our stories." Kaitlyn thought of her own story; how she wished her mother could see her now. "I believe all of us can lead epic lives as individuals and teams, not just for ourselves, but for the world around us. This is our promise. This is our code."

An image of her team came up on the screen. Every member held an animal.

"Students of Flint Hill," Kaitlyn said, "we call ourselves Code 7."

Samantha's song faded as the screen went black.

The room was still for a moment, and then it filled with thunderous applause. The crowd began to chant, "Code 7, Code 7, Code 7!"

Kaitlyn let out a breath and smiled.

I did it, Mom.

"Looks like we have a winner," Principal Cooler said. "Code 7 has just won themselves a pizza party!"

Kaitlyn's teammates jumped from their seats and gave each other big hugs. No one cared about the prize. What they had accomplished in the space of a week was far bigger than that.

"This makes me wonder," Sebastian said as he slapped Kaitlyn a high-five. "What are we going to do next?"

"Extreme sports!" suggested Talmage.

Kaitlyn laughed just as Genevieve gave her a hug. "You were great," Genevieve said. Kaitlyn smiled as she rested her chin on Genevieve's shoulder; it had been a long time since she had gotten a hug from a friend.

Kaitlyn glanced at the messenger bag resting in her seat. *I've changed people's minds about something, haven't I?*

But it wasn't leading people to care about homeless dogs and cats that made Kaitlyn so proud.

She had changed; she was no longer alone.

She was Kaitlyn again.

She had become ...

... Kaitlyn ... at last.

Visit the Code 7 website to learn more about the author and the story behind the stories!

www.CandyWrapper.co

Become a registered member of Code 7

Download the Discussion Guide

Learn more about Code 7 Challenges

Get a sneak preview of other books written by Bryan R. Johnson

CPSIA information can be obtained
at www.ICGtesting.com
Printed in the USA
LVHW111926230622
721975LV00002B/75

9 781940 556048